SNOW DUSK

ANAGH V

Contents

CHAPTER I

The Detective at Snowfields

8th December, 07:22PM, Snowfields.

"Two lone twinkling lights on a blue police van, travelling in the deserted Snowfields at dusk. Doesn't that seem insecure, sir?"

"..."

"Sir?"

"You don't feel insecure when you know there's no threat here"

"It's true, sir, but with this guy in the van..."

"That's why he is chained to his seat. And soon he will be chained to the rods of prison"

Noise is heard from the back of the van.

"Everything alright back there, officer?"

"Yes sir"

"...

Status, Alpha two point one. Over"

"About 35 kilometers more to the prison. Over"

"Copy that"

"The weather's a little eerie, don't you think, sir?"

"It is..."

"Come in, Alpha two point one. Blizzard warning, north-east of you. Acknowledge"

"Copy that"

"You better hurry, Alpha two point one"

"Yeah, we better do. We need to reach before the blizzard hits"

Hits, grunts and groans are heard from behind, "Stand back. Back!... Ah!!"

The van is stopped with a jerk.

"Are we alright, boys?"

"..."

The door is opened and the officer runs forward with a gun.

"Alpha two point one, come in"

"..."

"Alpha two point one. Come in!"

"..."

This is Alpha two point one... the prisoner has escaped! I repeat, Nathaniel has escaped! We need reinforcements!"

8th December, 7:49PM, Snowfields.

'This is Alpha two point one... the prisoner has escaped! I repeat, Nathaniel has escaped! We need reinforcements!' okay, on reading this, I get that the prisoner's name is Nathaniel. Well, there is not much narration there. Just conversation. So, not much information. Reading the escape isn't of much help', thought the detective.

The blue jeep was in front of him, with its head lights beaming on his jacket, leaving his face in darkness. 'No clues from the jeep too' he thought.

"Why didn't you chase him?" he asked the police officer beside him.

"Our men were badly hurt, sir. He ran away so fast that he was out of sight till we knew what was happening", replied the officer.

The cold winds were blowing fiercer.

"Can you keep this escape a secret and not let the public know?" asked the detective.

"Few villagers went this way, sir. They already know it" replied the officer, 'I should tell him that his name is Nathaniel', he thought, "Detective—"

"Please don't call me by my name, officer. Keeping it a secret might turn out to be useful. And yes, I know his name is Nathaniel"

The officer is astonished and puzzled.

"You said that he went north-east, right?" said the detective, looking through his binoculars, "it's completely foggy that way" he saw.

"Yes sir. But I should warn you, there's a—"

"A blizzard coming that way? Well, that should slow Nathaniel down and make him stay at a shelter. He possibly cannot pass through a blizzard. I'm going that way to catch him" declared the detective.

The officer, still totally confused, "Sir, you can't go one on one with him. He's too strong"

"Is there any other detective available who can accompany me?" the detective asked.

"Can't I or another officer accompany you?"

"No, Nathaniel's already seen you and obviously your uniform would give us away"

"I can contact detective Dusk. It might take him two hours or so to come"

"I'll better find Nathaniel first before he comes then", the detective got in his car.

The officer asked, "How will you both identify each other there? You and detective Dusk"

"We haven't seen each other anytime before. But I will know if it is him" the detective replied, thinking, 'I can read detective Dusk's thoughts once he enters into this book'

"But how?"

"That's the spell in two detectives talking" said the detective and drove off.

8th December, 8:21PM, Ice Lake Basin

The winds were blowing faster, just as Madhav had started to feel. He dug his feet into the depth of the snow, trying to walk faster. The heavy snow fell on his back. A moment later, a bright light, visible dim by the fierce snow was found at about a dozen meters.

'Ah, shelter!' Madhav said to himself and walked his way through the blizzard to the light. It was becoming clearer as he went forward – it looked like an abandoned old house, with sure good amount of electric pathway, standing alone in the blizzard, helplessly. Madhav could see a small room inside with red furniture, just as he stepped on the first elevation of wood. The wind would've thrown him away if he wouldn't have caught hold of the wooden bar for support.

'Finally. Wood feels a lot safer' he thought and looked into the house from the glass of the front door. The furniture looked warm and comfortable. Just as he touched the door knob, a voice from inside the room, was faintly heard.

"Yes, I have heard—"

"The prisoner—"

Madhav waited at the door knob for a moment, thinking. Then he scoffed and entered in. There were two men, sitting in sofas in the dim-lighted room. They both looked at Madhav, while he pushed off the snow from his coat.

"Hello there" one of them said.

"Oh, hi, it always feels good to see someone else when one's stuck in this kind of storm" said Madhav.

"Well, now we're three" said the man smiling, "I am Nathan"

'Okay, this man doesn't hesitate to reveal his identity' Madhav thought. "Oh! My name is Madhav" he said, walking to Nathan. 'Why am I even bothering? The prisoner escape could just even be a rumor' he thought, while he shook hands with Nathan.

"James" the other man said and shook his hands too.

Madhav took his coat off and placed himself in a seat that is a little away from James's. As he observed around him, the small room was only lit with three bulbs here and there and the chimney fire, the furniture was dusted, yet comfortable. A hallway seemed to be leading into darkness. It was warm but the huge glass-paned window showed the cold storming just outside the wall.

"You have never come here before, have you?" asked Nathan, "I can see that by the expression on your face"

"Yeah, it is my first time coming this way" Madhav replied, smiling.

"Your first time, you say?" James asked with a little suspicious tone.

Madhav looked at his face and his eyebrows were twisted a little. 'I just made myself suspicious of the prisoner, damn it' he thought. He gulped down his throat as he said, "I mean, I live at the East Horizon. I have come here to meet my professor"

Nathan's eyes widened, "The East Horizon? You got to be kidding me"

'This guy is getting me more suspicions even though I'm being honest' Madhav thought.

"I thought the blizzard has already swept up the place" exclaimed Nathan, "Didn't it originate from there?"

"No" Madhav said, "I've heard it comes from the south-west"

"Oh, these directions and the map!" Nathan said, "I am not so well in those. Being a student, it's a good thing that you know them"

Madhav smiled, 'There. That should remove the suspicion on me'

'Hmm...' James was thinking, 'There is no need to narrate me, author. I can break the fourth wall. SO yes, I am the detective at the Snowfields. I was following Nathaniel and ended up here, unable to escape from the blizzard. Although, I have a good feeling that Nathaniel might be one of these. From reading the thoughts of Madhav, I am a seventy per cent sure that he is not Nathaniel. I have been talking to Nathan. He, himself, brought up the topic but he thinks that it is just a rumor... Do you hear that? Hold on a second'

"Do you hear that?" James asked.

"Yeah, sounds like a car horn" Madhav replied.

They looked at each other's faces and immediately rushed out through the door.

"There! I see the car. It seems stuck in the snow" screamed Nathan to make his voice audible over the cold winds.

Two man-like figures emerged from inside the car. They began to run towards the shelter, stumbling in the snow. Madhav saw them from under a roof, just outside the warm room.

"We should help them!" he shouted and took a few steps into the snow, trying to offer a hand to the stranger who was sprinting towards him. As he neared, Madhav narrowed his eyes on the man's hands. He seemed to be carrying something – a dark solid. 'Is that a... gun?'

CHAPTER II

The Fourth Wall Breaks Twice

8th December, 8:01PM, Frozen Dune

Ashton was driving his car through the snow. 'It seems the storm is beginning' he thought, 'I need to wait this storm out at a shelter. Wait a minute. There was a shelter in the previous scene, where was it?... yes, Ice Lake Basin. I could go there and wait with those people. Yes, I break the fourth wall too. Maybe that car in the previous scene is mine—was mine?—will be mine?... Whatever'

A moment later, in the light of the car's headlights, he saw a man standing on the roadside, asking for lift. 'Poor guy! He might get stuck in the coming blizzard. I have to help him. However, the second person who stepped out of the car might be this guy' Ashton thought and stopped his car. The man asked Ashton for a lift to the village. Ashton nodded his head and the man got into the backseat of the car. The car started moving again.

"I'm Ashton"

"Oh, I am Gustavus" said the man comforting himself from the cold, "Thank you"

After a few moments of silence, Gustavus asked, "Are you new here? I've never seen you around"

"Um... yeah" Ashton said, eyes still fixed to the road.

'My friends were talking of an escaped prisoner. This guy seems suspicious' Gustavus thought.

'This guy is suspecting me, even though I'm not what he thinks I am. I should do something to remove that suspicion on me' thought Ashton. "But I visit my father's house here once in a while. I think the storm is getting worse. There must be a shelter here somewhere, right?" he said.

"Yes, that's a good idea" Gustavus replied. 'This guy knows the old coffee shop here, which means he isn't lying. He might not be the prisoner after all' he thought.

'That settled' Ashton thought again, 'Actually, this Gustavus guy must be the actual prisoner- what was his name? Nathaniel, huh. But Nathaniel might not have known this place clearly as Gustavus does' he accelerated the car as the snow howled louder, 'Or what if Nathaniel was native to this place and he escaped right here because he could hide among the people?'

Ashton stopped as he reached the shelter. 'Oh this looks darker than the way the author narrated it!' he thought. He honked the car twice and got out. "Come on!" he screamed to Gustavus.

Gustavus got something in his hand and got out of the car. They both started running to the shelter, stumbling on their way as the snow was thick. Ashton could see a few men running out from the front door and looking at them. One of them moved towards Gustavus and offered him a hand. But as Gustavus leaned forward to hold his hand, the man moved away backwards, probably in fear, falling into the snow.

James helped Madhav stand, while Nathan pulled Ashton and Gustavus from the snow and they hurried inside for warmth. Nathan shut the door behind him.

Ashton and Gustavus gasped for air and shook the snow off their coats.

"Damn, that's fierce!" Ashton exclaimed.

Madhav quickly took down Gustavus and pulled his hands back. Gustavus fell down on his knees and grunted in pain. All the others gasped and moved away. Madhav looked at Gustavus's hands. It was a cap – a black cap.

Nathan dragged Madhav away as he let go of Gustavus's hands.

"What are you doing?" Nathan asked.

"Nothing, I'm sorry, I thought I saw something else in his hands" Madhav moved away.

"What did you think you saw?"

'A gun' Ashton told himself.

"Umm... a gun" Madhav said slowly.

"What?" Gustavus exclaimed.

"I don't know! It was dark outside and something was in your hands and I thought it was a gun!" Madhav started to look panicked.

"Why would you think I had a gun?" roared Gustavus. He was definitely angry about it.

"I'm sorry I shouldn't have acted like that. I apologize" Madhav said and calmed Gustavus down. "I'm Madhav"

"Gustavus"

Everyone came back to ease.

'Okay, this Madhav guy looks suspicious' thought Ashton, 'Could he be the prisoner? He might've thought it was a gun, as he was afraid of the detective. Or could he be the detective himself? No, a detective wouldn't take such sudden decisions, thinking the suspect is indeed the prisoner. Or he could be a common man, afraid if Gustavus could be the prisoner. It could also be that he might have really seen the gun, which Gustavus really has. But I have so far not noticed something like a gun with Gustavus. However, Gustavus seems to be native. But he came out of literal nowhere, asking for lift. I need to observe each person more carefully'

'This Madhav is not so nice. He offers me a hand outside and suddenly pounces on me like I was a runaway thief' thought Gustavus, 'Or maybe he is a police officer trying to catch the escaped prisoner? I'm not sure about that'

'I shouldn't have acted like that. I don't care about the embarrassment. What concerns me more is that now they may suspect me as the prisoner, who is being cautious of the police' thought Madhav.

'Alright, this silence is creeping me out' thought Nathan. He said, "So, Ashton and Gustavus, you are both friends?"

"No, we actually just met a few minutes ago" replied Ashton.

"He gave me a lift in his car" said Gustavus, "What about you, Nathan?"

Nathan said "Oh, I've come here before any of you. This once was owned by my grandfather. It was a coffee shop. I used to play as a child here..."

'Nathan is the only one with a cool head here' thought Ashton, 'Maybe he is naive or he is a good actor'.

At the same time James was also thinking the same. 'Everyone here is only suspecting that the others could be the prisoner, except Nathan. Also no one has implied that they are the prisoner in their thoughts, or at least in the thoughts that the author decided to mention'

".... and so, I come here sometimes to relive few good memories..." Nathan was continuing.

'And there is this other fourth wall breaker in the room' both thought it at the same time and looked at each other suddenly. Their eyes were fixed, not a blink.

Three Variables

'James says that he is the detective'

'Ashton says he's not the prisoner'

"... and that's how my grandfather sold this coffee shop" finished Nathan.

"Look at that SNOW! It is covering my car!" said Ashton, alarmed. The word 'snow' was louder and clearer. "Isn't it James?"

"Yes, it is" James replied, a bit confused. 'Why did this guy ask only me?'

Ashton had a slight smirk.

'I told this whole story and all they care about is the car!' Nathan rustled inside.

James seemed to set his hair and then gave a piercing look at Ashton that looked like a lightning.

"Where did you say you were from, Ashton?" asked James.

"From the Salt Banks", Ashton replied, "I ride here sometimes to see my mother".

'He said 'father' to me' thought Gustavus.

"... and my father. They both live together here at the Ice Lake Basin".

"So, you have come to see your parents and got caught in this blizzard", said Nathan.

"No, actually I am here to see my father. My mother, she had to go to the city on her work", replied Ashton, still looking at James, who was looking back at him.

'What is up with these two guys?' Gustavus thought "They are just staring at each other without even a blink.

These might know each other. Actually, these both might be the two escaped prisoners.'

'Two prisoners! Rumors do carry false news every time' James thought.

'Given the fact that everyone is keeping silent and staring weird, the prisoner must definitely be among us', Madhav thought 'Before I was here, James and Nathan were talking about the prisoner but they stopped immediately when I walked in. Could they both be the prisoners? Or they could both be police officers, here to find the prisoners. Either way, I have to be cautious on not making myself suspicious of the prisoner".

Meanwhile, Ashton was thinking, 'The police officer at Snowfields seemed to describe the prisoner as muscly and strong. James, Gustavus and Madhav – all of them look quite strong'

Suddenly Gustavus stomach growled, "Oh! Sorry" he exclaimed with a short laugh.

"Seems like you are hungry" said Madhav, with a smile.

"Yes" replied Gustavus, with a serious look at Madhav, "I haven't eaten in the evening"

'The prisoner wouldn't have eaten anything in the evening and as Ashton said, he was in the middle of the road, with no transport at all. He could be the one' thought James, 'the author didn't mention anything about how Gustavus reached there'

"Actually, I have a few rotis left. You can have them" said Madhav, searching his bag. He took out a steel box from it, opened it and gave it to Gustavus.

'This guy is nice' thought Ashton.

'If he is the prisoner, he wouldn't have had this food' Gustavus took the box. "Thank you" he smiled.

"Can I have some too?" asked James.

"Yeah, sure" Madhav said with a short laugh.

Gustavus opened the tin, "Oh, chicken!" he said with excitement.

Both of them began eating. Nathan looked at Ashton, "You want some?"

"No, I am a vegetarian", Ashton declined.

"That explains why you are skinny", said Nathan, grinning, taking another bite at the roti, "Just kidding, but you should try chicken at least once, man"

Ashton just smiled as a reply.

He stood up and moved towards the huge window. He put his hands back and held one in another and looked through the window. The storm outside was unforgiving. As snow poured down, there was no creature seen on the…

'No author, I am not observing the storm', Ashton whispered. He was looking at the other four in the reflection of the glass. They were all eating.

'We have four people here and three variables – The detective, the prisoner, and another detective named Dusk. Gustavus is being quite and conservative. He seems to be native here, yet he was all alone in the middle of the blizzard when I found him. I could ask him what he was doing there, but he already suspects me for the prisoner. I better not make myself look like the prisoner, when I'm not. Madhav acted weird, thinking of gun in Gustavus's hands in a way that a prisoner would react on seeing a detective. Nathan is the last person to be a prisoner, he seems to be naive and extrovert, something a prisoner on the run wouldn't be. But Madhav saw him and James talking about the prisoner. Oh, James! The guy who can even read what I am thinking right now'

Just then, James glanced at Ashton for a second and leaned further in his seat, stretching his legs.

'He says that he is the detective and there should be another detective named Dusk' thought Ashton. "The snow doesn't seem to slow down. I think we will be spending the whole night here" he said out loud.

"Yeah, maybe", replied Nathan and stood up. He walked towards Ashton and looked out of the window. The storm was still raging.

"But, sometimes the storms forgive. They halt for a small two to five minutes gap and then they continue with the same ferocity. We could run to a place nearby if we want in that gap", he said still looking out of the window.

"But that happens only sometimes" Gustavus replied. 'The prisoner could use the gap to run and hide in some place' he thought.

'But there would be no place nearby for the prisoner to hide, which is a better hiding spot than this shelter' James thought.

Madhav closed the box and put it inside his bag. He was thinking 'I don't know what crime the prisoner had done. It might be a murder or a robbery or something else. The prisoner could be ruthless. He could be savage. Sweat dropped from his forehead. 'No, I need to have courage. He wouldn't strike when there are four other people'.

While Gustavus thought 'Why is this guy sweating in this ice-cold blizzard?'

"It's been an hour since we are here" James said.

"If you are getting bored, we all could play a game" Nathan said, "There are dice and tin boxes in the next room. I can bring them. Anyone wants to go with me?"

The other just looked each other faces but no one replied.

'If Nathan is the prisoner, then going with him alone would be terrible idea' thought Madhav.

'If Nathan is the prisoner, I could, maybe, confirm it by going with him or I could see if he is the detective Dusk' thought James, 'But he seemed like neither when I first talked to him'. "I'll come" he replied.

"Nice, follow me" Nathan said and began walking into the dark hallway. James followed him into the darkness. Madhav thought, 'These both were talking about the prisoner until I arrived but they immediately stopped on seeing me. Now, they both are into the darkness together. Something is fishy between them'

While Gustavus's thoughts were on Ashton. 'If Ashton was the prisoner, he couldn't have a car. Even if he stole someone else's car, he wouldn't have stopped for me in the first place. That would just increase his risk of getting caught as I might have been a detective'. But Ashton's thoughts were elsewhere.

"Why isn't the author narrating what is happening between James and Nathan? What is going on between them?" He kept looking at the dark hallway.

"If one of them is a prisoner, something might happen in that room. Gustavus and Madhav do not seem like the prisoners and they don't seem like they are detectives too. Or...' He paused.

"May be I have been thinking all wrong about this. May be the prisoner is another fourth wall breaker but is acting like he's not. He might have been reading all this and acting accordingly. And whatever he thinks as a prisoner, the author might not be writing them. The author might be aiding the prisoner. Why would the author aid the bad guy? Isn't this a 'good wins against bad' story? What other stories did this author write? 'Tracks Go Mad'— just a happy-to-go story, doesn't relate to the current situation. 'The Avarez Theft'— the story where good people perform a bank heist for a good reason. Could that mean the prisoner here might be a good guy?' He closed his eyes and put his hands on his temple. 'I'm just overthinking this. The detective at Snowfields seemed pretty confident on catching the prisoner. But, I must say, the prisoner seems to be playing it really smart'.

Suddenly, there were footsteps heard, coming from the hallway. Madhav, Gustavus and Ashton were waiting with their eyes fixed into the darkness. Thunder rumbled outside. Soon, a man walked into the room. It was James.

CHAPTER IV

Liar's Dice

"Where's Nathan?" asked Ashton.

"He is right behind" replied James and Nathan also emerged from the darkness.

"There are enough dice for all of us" said Nathan and put them on the table.

Looking at the twisted eyebrows of Madhav, James asked him, "Is everything all right Madhav?"

Madhav immediately turned his face and said, "Yeah, everything is good. It's just that... the... blizzard is getting worse"

"Yeah, but we at least have something to play" replied James. 'Madhav is really concerned about who the prisoner is. Could he be detective Dusk?' he thought, 'He fears too much. Maybe he is just an afraid, common man'.

"Let's play 'Liar's dice' game", said Nathan.

Everyone was seated around the table. Madhav sat against the large window, while Gustavus sat against the dark hallway. James sat against Ashton. 'Nathan does know a whole lot about this coffee shop. Maybe what he said about him visiting this place every now and then is true' thought Gustavus.

"The rules are simple. You will have five dice in each of your cups. We roll the dice, keeping it concealed. One person bids, announcing any face value and the minimum number of dice that the player believes, are showing that value, under all of the cups in the game. The next player either increases the bid or challenges the previous bid by calling him 'liar'" explained Nathan.

'Nathan and James, both seem the same after coming out. If Nathan told James something secret, James would act somewhat weird and vice versa. But Nathan is still enthusiastic and talking too much and James is still... well, looking creepy and suspicious. Either they both already knew something and talked more about it or they talked no secret at all' thought Ashton.

"What are you thinking, Ashton?" asked James, "It's your turn"

"Oh! Yeah, didn't see that" he said, "What is your bid again, Gustavus?"

"Four fives"

"Well then, I bid four sixes"

8th December, 10:46 PM.

"I bid nine sixes" said James.

"Are you sure?" asked Madhav, "Just so you know, I might not have any sixes"

"No, I'm sure" replied James.

"Then, I call you liar" said Madhav. The cups were opened and there were nine sixes indeed.

"I had all of my dice fall six. That's like really rare, right?" exclaimed James.

"You have already won four rounds. You seem so good at this game, James" said Gustavus. James simply smiled.

"Where are you from, James?" Gustavus asked.

"I'm from... Northern Gates" said James. 'Ashton knows I'm lying because he knows that I am the detective. Shoot!' he thought. "I've come to see a dear friend of mine here, at Snowfields" he said, gazing right into the eyes of Ashton.

"Well then, how did you end up here?" asked Ashton.

"My friend was not there. So I asked his neighbor and he told me that he went to Ice Lake Basin but he didn't know why" he said, still looking at Ashton and rolling his dice. "I'm here to find him" he said, uttering every word specifically and with a little serious tone, "But now, I'm stuck in this blizzard" he came back to his usual accent, "My bid is four threes"

'He is referring to the prisoner', Ashton thought. "So, when you were at Snowfields, did you hear of a prisoner escape?" asked Gustavus, slowly.

"What! Are you really believing that rumor?" laughed Nathan, "Four sixes"

"No, no. it's not a rumor", said James.

Gustavus and Madhav felt alert. "What?" asked Nathan.

"I've seen it. I've seen the police there, talking about a prisoner", replied James calmly.

Everyone went silent for a few moments.

'So it's real' Madhav thought.

Nathan's face suddenly turned blue. He gulped and he was sweating.

'If the prisoner is real then he must have reached here' thought Nathan, 'He must be one among us. There is no other way out from the Snowfields'. He rubbed the sweat from his forehead.

The snowstorm roared even louder and thunder struck once more.

'James could have told me that he has seen it when we first talked about the prisoner, but he didn't' Nathan thought. "Why didn't you tell me about this before, James?" he asked.

"Well, I didn't feel the need to tell it", replied James, "It's not like the prisoner is among us, right?" he laughed, 'I'd like to see how everyone reacts'

"Yes, probably not" replied Ashton, with no emotion in his face at all. 'Well, all of us know, that obviously, the prisoner is right among us', he thought.

Madhav kept his head down; Gustavus was looking at everyone; Nathan was the most shocked. He closed his eyes for two seconds and opened them in fear and was constantly rubbing his palms gently.

"Five fours" said Ashton after a long silence.

The others kept quiet, thinking. They were not willing to continue playing after the conversation that took place.

They frequently looked at each other— some were the looks of fear, while some were the looks of suspicion.

'The author is not narrating their thoughts except Nathan's' thought James, 'That's a bit mysterious'.

"Come on, Nathan. Your turn now, five fours" Ashton said with a stable expression in his face.

Nathan thought for a moment or two and looked at Ashton, "four sixes" he said.

The game continued.

"Ashton doesn't seem very affected by the conversation. Everyone else looks pretty scared or suspecting" James thought, 'Could Ashton be the prisoner? He does feel very suspicious'

Ashton looked at James. James looked back at him. Gustavus looked at them eye each other and thought 'These two might be the two escaped prisoners. They stare at each other every time. They might be talking to each other through signs. But James was already here before I and Ashton arrived. Also, Ashton wouldn't have a car if he were the prisoner too. Then why are they frequently eyeing one another? I need to observe more...'

'This is causing new suspicions, damn it' James thought, "Five sixes".

Everything was quiet then, except for the rumble of the wind on a glass window of the room. The game continued with increasing intensity. Slowly, all of them were involved in it. But James was partially still out of the game. 'I keep thinking, why is this story named 'SNOW DUSK?' Does it mean the snow pours down until the dusk quits? That can't be good then. Well, we know there's a detective dusk in the story. So, does it mean he is going to be covered in snow? Or he uses snow to catch the prisoner? In anyway, the snow is going to play a major role here I need to keep an eye on that' he thought. He gazed at Ashton.

Ashton was busy in the game "Six sixes", but James knew that Ashton knew what he was thinking.

'He doesn't seem to be worried about the title. Either he knows what it means or the author's not writing what he's thinking. The second option worries me more'.

CHAPTER V

Blinding Lights

"Do you know what crime the prisoner committed?" Ashton asked James.

"I, uh... have no idea about that"

"Hmm..."

"Liar!" Gustavus called. The cups were lifted. There weren't six sixes in total. "Yes!"

"Alright. Another game"

They reshuffled the dice.

"Four fours" Nathan said.

"That's a big bid to start with" Madhav said, "And you know what? I am fine with that. Five fours"

'Ashton is damn suspicious' James thought.

"James, it's your turn".

"Six fours" James said. 'It feels Ashton might actually be the prisoner' he thought.

"LIAR!!" Ashton cried.

"Huh?"

"Liar, there aren't six fours" Ashton said.

"Oh!"

There weren't six fours. "James is very suspicious" Gustavus said out loud. Everyone looked at him with a paused breath. "He always gets to be the liar". All of them exhaled at once.

"Another match?"

Suddenly, the sound of the wind hitting the glass window of the room stopped and the lights went out and came on all at a moment

"Huh?"

"What happened?"

No one answered the question. Everyone kept rolling their eyes at all of the room's light. They were all as quite as mice. There was a loud thunder suddenly and everything went dark again. There were no loud winds outside as if the storm wasn't there at all.

"What happened?" growled Gustavus. Nothing could be seen. "Everybody, stand back!" shouted Nathan in an agonizing voice. 'The prisoner, whoever it is, might hit me, or worse, shoot me in this darkness' thought Nathan. He was very afraid and moved back as far as he could, until he hit a wall.

'It seems to be the break of the blizzard. The storm stops for a few minutes now' thought Madhav and suddenly he heard a large sound as the table fell down, 'Oh! The prisoner is here!' he cried out loud inside of him and ran back.

'These three are here and are worried' thought Ashton, 'Where is James?'

"James!" he shouted.

'I knew Ashton and James were working together as prisoners. They are gonna kill us' thought Gustavus and was terrified completely, "Nooo!" he shouted.

There was silence outside but everyone was hearing their own heart thumping and was knocking things down in fear. 'I shouldn't let James escape' Ashton thought and rushed to the last place where he saw James.

Suddenly the lights came back and they were flickering. The noises all stopped as everybody stopped moving. In that flickering, Ashton could see them— Nathan, was at the far end, backed to a wall, almost in tears; Gustavus was at the window, also afraid to the toe; Madhav was on the floor with his palms tightly pressing his ears in fear.

'James...' Ashton turned around. James was standing in the place where Ashton previously was, not at all looking scared. He looked back at him with his eyebrows twisted. They looked at each other for a moment.

"What happened?" asked James, turning to the others.

"It is probably the break of the blizzard" said Madhav slowly, trying to stand up and look normal.

'The break?' James thought. Everything was silent outside, but still freezing. There was hardly any light in the room and the one that was left was strongly flickering. Gustavus looked out the window. It almost looked like a wounded warrior fallen in war.

"Everything's calm outside" he said.

"We better leave before the blizzard comes back then" James said.

"No" Madhav urged, "We won't make it. The storm will be back in about five minutes. There is no way we'll make it out by then. If we don't cross the storm before it resumes, we will be frozen to death"

'It's better if I go out in a storm than get blocked in a room knowing there's an assassin here' thought Gustavus. The light flickered hard.

"Are you sure we can't manage to get out?" asked James, "I can't stay here any longer".

"No way" said Madhav, "There is no shelter anywhere near, and we can't cross the blizzard before it starts again"

Everyone was standing at random points in the room.

"How about Ashton's car? We could go faster with that" asked Nathan.

"I'm sure we will have a good time finding it five miles under the snow" said Ashton.

"How long do you suppose we stay here then?" Gustavus asked.

"About half the time that has passed" Madhav said in a low voice. The room was in silence.

The flickering lights blinded Ashton.

"What's with the lights?" he asked.

"The transition of the storm might have damaged the generator" Nathan said.

'There's a generator here? A working one?' Madhav thought.

"Where's the generator?"

Nathan pointed to the hallway connected to the room.

"If it really is damaged, we need to get it back working. I know how to, but someone else must come with me"

"Well then, someone can go along with Nathan to the generator" Ashton said.

Everyone just looked at each other. They knew that the others were thinking the same that they were thinking. The silence continued.

'I must go to the generator. The person who comes with me matters. Gustavus might be the prisoner. I hope he doesn't come' Nathan thought.

'Nathan knows the way. So he must go. I don't think Nathan is the prisoner but I am afraid if Nathan is indeed the prisoner, I might never come out from the hallway' Madhav thought.

'James's got to be the prisoner. He asked Madhav the most number of times if he could go out. Madhav's got to be the detective, since he didn't want anyone to escape. That might also be the reason why he took me down at the first time. I better stay with Madhav. Hope he doesn't go with Nathan' Gustavus thought.

'If Nathan is indeed the prisoner, I would be in trouble if I go with him. Although he is the least I would suspect, if he really is, the prisoner, I will be knocked out. He indeed looks like the strongest among us. It would be better if I stayed with the others, one of whom might be the prisoner. I wonder what James is planning to do' Ashton thought

'I was watching Nathan from the beginning. He was the one who acted all the time as if he was trying to make everyone believe that there is, after all, no prisoner at all. He should be the prisoner. I'm sure of it. I should go with him, just in case he escapes from the back', James thought, 'However, if the prisoner is one of the left behind, he wouldn't try to escape with two other men watching'

"I'll come" he said.

The other four looked at him sternly.

"Okay" Nathan said, almost thankful that it was not Gustavus, who was vouching to go.

James walked towards Nathan. They whispered to each other. Nathan nodded and looking at the others, said, "We'll go now". They started walking into the dark hallway connected to the room. All of this made Ashton feel uncomfortable. Gustavus was feeling quite safe with Madhav with him.

James and Nathan were walking.

"How far is the generator?" James asked.

"About a minute, that's it" Nathan replied, "But the further we go in, the darker and colder it becomes"

"Why is that so?" James asked.

"The lights over there were already damaged by such snow storm, years ago"

"Oh"

They walked cautiously. There were dark rooms on the side of the hallway, everything quiet.

Back in the hall, Gustavus, Madhav and Ashton, sat far away from each other, all quiet. Nobody wanted to talk. Instead, everyone was thinking hard. Every moment James and Nathan don't return, new thoughts arose in their mind.

"Is there any opening from the back, Nathan?" James asked. Nathan was walking silently. He looked at James without turning his head. He could see dark and heavy boots walking. Nathan gulped. 'Why is he asking this question?'

"Nathan?" James increased his voice.

"There is one at the generator." Nathan replied.

'Why does James need to know if there is a way out?' Ashton thought.

James could see a wall at the end of the hallway, after silently walking for a while.

"We're here" Nathan said.

James observed that there was a door on the right.

'No' Ashton said to himself and almost got up from his seat.

"Something wrong, Ashton?" Madhav asked.

"No, nothing, heh" Ashton stammered as he spoke.

Madhav twisted his eyebrows. 'Is Ashton the prisoner? Was he trying to escape through the door, now?'

Nathan opened the door, leading to the open Ice Lake Basin. He stepped into the snow, cautiously. James also stepped out. The generator was just by the door. Nathan kept an eye on James, who was looking at the snow beyond, but not at the generator. Nathan felt unsafe.

Suddenly, James twisted his eyebrows and immediately leaped forward with steps.

'What! Is James the prisoner?! He's escaping!' Nathan thought.

CHAPTER VI

Two Detectives Talking

'No!!' Ashton got up and stood on his legs.

'No!' Nathan immediately turned around and held out his hand to try and get hold of James from escaping. There, he saw James stop at the end of the wooden elevation, holding out his hand. He also saw another manly- figure in a jacket.

The man stepped on to the wood with the help of James's hand.

Madhav and Gustavus also stood partially as a defense reflex. Ashton fell back into his seat, looking at them who looked back at him, to let him know that he was very suspicious.

James thought in his mind 'Wow. And I just played police before the real one'. He looked at Nathan's strange behaviour.

"What's wrong, Nathan?"

"Nothing, I... I was just asking you for help" Nathan replied, rather nervously.

The stranger stopped panting and looked at James and Nathan. 'Okay... Two people here. Let's hope I get the sufficient time to find which one of them is the prisoner' he thought, 'and also, there's detective Snow among these. He might be waiting for me. I need to find him too'.

'Whaat!?' James thought, and suddenly looked at the man.

"Whaat!? Ashton thought, with his eyes raised.

'So this guy is the other detective?' James thought.

'I can convince him that I am the detective... uh... Snow. Then I'll find a way'.

"Hello, I am James" he said.

"Hi. Daktar" the man replied and shook his hand with James's.

"Hi Daktar, I am Nathan" said Nathan from the generator, "James, I said I need your help here!"

James reluctantly stepped on the snow towards Nathan.

'Nathan? It's very close to 'Nathaniel'. Hmm... but a prisoner might not choose such a name if he wants himself in disguise. I also need to know if there are only two of these here to come to a conclusion. First, is this the shelter that I am told?'

"Daktar, it's the break of the blizzard. How are you able to reach here?" Nathan asked cautiously, thinking, 'Surely, the prisoner *was* among us? Or were all of us innocent and this guy is the actual prisoner!?'

"Oh, I came in my car. It's over there" Daktar talked cautiously, "It broke down and I thought I could take shelter here"

Nathan looked to find a car far away.

"Daktar, I know the look in your face. This is the shelter you need at the time of the blizzard" James said, looking at him from the generator.

"I sure do hope I reached in time, I mean, before the blizzard continues" Daktar spoke cautiously, standing on the wood elevation.

"You have" James replied.

'Okay... this guy wants to talk. Could he be the detective?'

'No!!' Ashton could not hold his anxiety.

"Are only you two here?"

"Uh... no. There are three others. We've come here to fix the generator. It's been disturbed in the transition of the storm"

"Oh, really?" Daktar said.

Nathan grunted at the generator.

"Is it clear in the darkness? Or can I come and help?" Daktar asked.

"No, it's almost... over...uh..." Nathan grunted again. The generator grunted and hissed.

"There it starts" Nathan said with half contentment.

"Now let's go in"

The flickering lights in the room became stiff and bright all of a sudden. 'Nathan might've fixed the generator' thought Gustavus.

Nathan and James jumped back on the wood.

"Follow us, Daktar" said Nathan and walked inside, followed by James and Daktar. Nathan closed the door behind them.

'Ah, I could've used Daktar's car! However, I've got another good opportunity with him' James thought.

"They are late, don't you think, Madhav?" Gustavus asked.

"They are" Madhav replied with a low tone. Both of them looked at Ashton, who sat in a sofa, silent to himself.

"So, Daktar" James wanted to talk to Daktar very badly.

"Yes?"

"It looked like you were coming from the Snowfields"

"Yes... yes I was"

"Then I do think you've heard of a prisoner on the run, haven't you?" James asked.

'Alright. James really wants to talk about this. He could either be the prisoner or the detective. I need to pin him and find out' Daktar thought.

"Yes, I have" he replied.

Nathan was carefully listening 'James's got to be the prisoner'.

'James might even succeed in convincing Daktar that he is the detective. I should not let him do that' Ashton thought.

"Hey, they really are being late. What if I go check out on them, huh?" he asked.

Madhav and Gustavus looked at Ashton. They did not find any difficulty with that decision of his. Gustavus nodded. "Okay. But be back" Madhav said 'Ashton's got to be the prisoner'

James was loading a conversation with Daktar in his mind.

Ashton stood and walked quickly towards the hallway, and stopped when he could see three manly-figures walking towards him. Nathan entered the room first, and then James, followed by Daktar.

Ashton and James caught each other's eye and fixed it. They eyed each other until Gustavus broke the silence in the room. Then Ashton saw Daktar. He felt supported all of a sudden.

"Woah, who's this?" Gustavus asked and stood up.

"Hi, I am Daktar" Daktar said, "I've come to take shelter here...". Ashton interrupted, "Well that's what we've all come here for, Daktar. I am Ashton"

"Madhav"

"Gustavus"

They shook hands.

They took their seats again, Nathan away from James and Madhav away from Ashton.

"From where do you come, Daktar?" Madhav asked.

"I..." Daktar was interrupted by James.

"He is from the Snowfields, am I right? We talked" James said, partially looking at Ashton and Daktar, "And, Daktar, you know, as per the news at the Snowfields, the escaped prisoner came this way and he might even be here".

Madhav and Gustavus looked at James uncomfortably.

'James looks more interested in this all of a sudden?'

"Yes, I heard the police say that", Daktar replied carefully.

"You were one of the villagers who saw the crime scene?" Ashton asked, acting if he was really interested.

"I was. I actually came here to visit a friend"

"I wasn't directly at the crime scene, but I got to know of it by one of the villagers who saw it. I got to know the detailed situation at the crime scene" James winked at Daktar.

"Oh, their head officer was so angry of the prisoner escape, that he banged and destroyed the siren lights of the police jeep, you know!" Daktar cautiously spoke with a low tone.

"Yes... yes, I was told of that. He might be really upset" James replied, slowly.

"Oh, James, you knew the details of the crime scene, but you hadn't told us any of this before?" Ashton interrupted, mockingly.

Nathan, Gustavus and Madhav saw the conversation quietly. They all detected that something was happening and did not want to interfere, but were ready to face any consequence.

'Okay, Ashton and James are fighting each other to gain my attention. One of them must be the prisoner and the other the detective' Daktar thought, 'Let's set things right'.

"However, James, the prisoner might not have come here in the blizzard" he said.

"I don't know, but I am sure that he might be powerful, as he was able to break out from police" James replied.

"Oh, truly, does this place always have such heavy SNOW here?" Daktar said, stressing at 'snow'.

A moment of silence.

"Yeah, it's been snowing today since DUSK" Ashton told Daktar with a smirk, "James, here, knows more about it"

James hesitantly gave away an awkward smile.

Ashton and Daktar eyed one another for a second or two. Everyone was quiet and still. All of a sudden, Ashton and Daktar put their hands on the back of their waists. Both of them pulled a gun out and with their arms stiff, stood up and pointed it to the head of James.

Everyone gasped and stood up in awe.

"Hands where I can see them, James... or should I say... Nathaniel" Daktar said loudly and sternly.

"Step back, Madhav. We are detective Snow and detective Dusk. We have the scene under our control" Ashton shouted, moving around James.

Nathan, Gustavus and Madhav were baffled.

'It was James all along!?'

James had his hands in the air, with a face full of confusion and anger.

"How did you know?"

"You said so yourself dummy . You played police before the real one" Ashton smiled.

James did not dare to move with two guns pointed at him.

Daktar took out his walkie-talkie from nowhere.

"Arena log eight. Come in. We've got the prisoner captured. I repeat— we've got Nathaniel captured. Waiting for reinforcements"

9th December, 2:07AM, Ice Lake Basin.

The prisoner was held with his hands tied back. The winds calmed down in the aftermath of the snowstorm.

Madhav, Nathan and Gustavus stood along with the detectives and the police officer. The three officers carrying the prisoner, stopped at the back of the police jeep.

The prisoner grunted.

"James" Detective Snow called. The prisoner, after a moment, with his head hung down, smiled lightly. He looked at the detective only with the eyes.

The detectives looked at the prisoner. "Anything to say?"

He raised his head and looked at the twinkling red and blue over the jeep.

"The siren lights aren't broken" he said.

Detective Dusk grinned.

The officers hurried the prisoner into the jeep, and the door was closed. The engine of the jeep rumbled coldly, as it set off with a cloud of fog.

"We thank you for your help in capturing the prisoner, detective" the officer said, "I just wonder how you came to know that he is detective Dusk"

Detective Snow smiled, "That's the spell in two detectives talking"